This book belongs to:

For a list of other books by Audrey Wood,
visit her Web site at: www.AudreyWood.com

LITTLE SIMON
An imprint of Simon & Schuster Children's Publishing Division
1230 Avenue of the Americas, New York, New York 10020
Copyright © 2001 by Audrey Wood
All rights reserved including the right of reproduction in whole or in part in any form.
LITTLE SIMON and colophon are registered trademarks of Simon & Schuster.
Manufactured in the United States of America
First Edition
2 4 6 8 10 9 7 5 3 1
ISBN 0-689-84347-X
Library of Congress Catalog Card Number 00-108424

A Book for Honey Bear

Reading Keeps the Sighs Away

by Audrey Wood

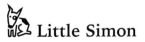 Little Simon

New York   London   Toronto   Sydney   Singapore

Honey Bear didn't feel well.

"Honey Bear!" Mama Bear said. "What's the matter? Why aren't you playing with your toys?"

"I don't want to," Honey Bear said. And then she sighed.

"Why don't you make a bear out of dough?" Papa Bear asked.

"I don't want to," Honey Bear said. And then she sighed again. . . .

"How about coloring or doing a puzzle?" Mama Bear said.
Honey Bear sighed a third time. Then she crawled into her bed, sat down, and pulled the covers over her head.

After a while Mama Bear said, "Something is wrong with Honey Bear."

Papa Bear pulled the covers down and felt the little bear's nose. "Her nose is hot!" he exclaimed.

This time Honey Bear sighed the longest sigh she had ever sighed.

"Oh, dear!" Papa Bear said. "I don't like the sound of those sighs. Doctor Bear must see her right away."

In the doctor's waiting room, Honey Bear couldn't stop sighing.

"Honey Bear!" the nurse called. "It's your turn now."

"Good afternoon, Honey Bear," Doctor Bear said. "What seems to be the matter?"

"I've got the sighs," Honey Bear said with a sigh.

"Honey Bear was sitting under her covers. Her nose was very hot," Papa Bear said.

"She didn't want to play with her toys, color, make bears out of dough, or put puzzles together," Mama Bear added.

Doctor Bear held Honey Bear's paws and looked into her eyes.

"Hmmm," he said.

Next, he took her temperature.

"Hmmm," the doctor said again, this time shaking his head.
Then he looked in her ears and mouth.

"This could be serious," he said.

The Bear family held their breath while the doctor thought.

"What's the matter with our Honey Bear?" Mama Bear cried.

"Ah, yes. I know!" the doctor said at last.

Doctor Bear took out a pad and wrote a note.
"Honey Bear needs a special prescription," he said. "Do
as I say every day, and she will be just fine."

The Bears hurried home and followed Dr. Bear's orders.
Papa Bear added extra pillows to their comfy couch.

Honey Bear picked out a tall stack of books. Then they all cuddled up together and followed the doctor's orders.